STEALING MACGUFFIN

This title is number four in the Frayed Edge Press Street Smart Series, published irregularly starting in 2019.

Other titles in the series include:

Full Fare by Jean-Bernard Pouy

Down and Out in Paris, with Cat by R.A. Bolo

The Accidental Anarchist by A.R. Melnik

Pele's Domain by Albert Tucher

STEALING MACGUFFIN

Matthew Kastel

Frayed Edge Press
Philadelphia, PA

Published by Frayed Edge Press in 2019

https://www.frayededgepress.com/

This book is printed on acid-free paper.

Interior illustrations by Bruce Orr

Publisher's Cataloging-in-Publication Data

Names: Kastel, Matthew.
Title: Stealing MacGuffin / Matthew Kastel.
Description: Philadelphia, PA : Frayed Edge Press, 2019. | Series: Street smart
    series ; 4 | Summary: A failed screenwriter turned private detective in Baltimore
    has his life turned upside-down when he's talked into stealing MacGuffin,
    an unusual Tinseltown memento, from the home of one of Hollywood's most
    infamous directors.
Identifiers: LCCN 2019955530 | ISBN 9781642510171 (pbk.) | ISBN
    9781642510188 (ebook)
Subjects: LCSH: Motion picture producers and directors -- Fiction. | Private
    investigators – Maryland – Baltimore – Fiction. | Theft -- Fiction. | Baltimore
    (Md.) -- Fiction. | BISAC: FICTION / Crime. | FICTION / Mystery & Detective
    / Hard-Boiled. | FICTION / Mystery & Detective / Private Investigators.
Classification: LCC PS3611.A88 S74 2019 | DDC 813 K38--dc23
LC record available at https://lccn.loc.gov/2019955530

Chapter One

Some people are born criminals. Others, like me, are drawn into criminal enterprise by opportunity. But for now, that was in my future.

I run a forgettable one-man detective agency that usually settles for the dregs of detective work: spying on cheap hotels to catch cheating spouses or freelancing for insurance companies to expose people on disability doing things like water skiing. I may not have followed all of life's rules, but theft was something I hadn't stooped to before. I was about to hit a new low.

I was sitting alone in a blue-collar bar near the Port of Baltimore awaiting the arrival of Bert Thompson. Yesterday, Bert had sent me a cryptic email saying he was in town from Hollywood and had some business to discuss with me. Bert and I go back to my Hollywood days. That's right. You heard me. My Hollywood days.

When I finished college, I fancied myself an up-and-coming screenwriter and traveled to Tinseltown to make a name for myself. I got a little studio apartment on Sunset that I had to bolt myself into at night to keep from getting robbed by the junkies and streetwalkers who took over the neighborhood from dusk to dawn.

I lived that way for a decade. To say that work was sporadic is an understatement. I have a few things to my credit on my IMDb page but not much. To survive, I worked all the typical jobs—waiter, light carpentry, cabbie. Then one day, my father begged me to come help him with the detective agency he was trying to get off the ground. He'd just been thrown off the Baltimore PD for being a raging alcoholic. I decided to chuck show business and moved back home to Baltimore. Six months later my old man checked out of life, and I was left in charge of a detective agency, a business I knew almost nothing about.

Bert, for a brief while, was my writing partner or the closest thing I had to a writing partner. He was a good decade older than me and had more contacts with agents and producers, so I thought we would be a good match. In the end I did ninety percent of the writing and although our partnership didn't produce much more of note than one episode of a mildly successful sitcom and a made-for-TV movie that never got on air, we still got some cash for them.

That was ten years ago. But as fate would have it, within a year of my breaking up the partnership and leaving Hollywood, Bert hit the big time when he penned an indie flick about a transvestite who backpacks across Europe and finds love. It was all the buzz at Cannes. There hasn't been a day since that I haven't wondered what my career could have been like if I'd stuck with him.

After Cannes Bert got a seven-figure deal to write the screenplay for a big studio movie, which promptly flopped at the box office. Since then, Bert raced through two actress wives, so I imagine most of the money is gone, especially seeing that his IMDb page shows he hasn't worked much in the last few years. Still, he had his moment.

It was a cold fall day, and I hadn't broken out my warm clothes yet, so each time the bar door was flung open, a chill rattled me to the bones. Eventually, the wind blew in a cold blast from my past in the figure of Bert Thompson.

Bert was a big man, standing well over six feet tall and beefy, which made him look strong rather than fat. We had exchanged a few emails over the years, but it had been a long time since I had seen him in the flesh. He hadn't changed much. He must have been about fifty now, and the only hint that he had aged since the last time I saw him was some graying around the temples.

We shook hands and Bert jingled. I should explain that Bert was one of those men who wore chains and rings to the point of ridicule. It's a Hollywood thing, I guess. He also had a cheesy black mustache that made him look like a character straight out of central casting for a '70s porno.

We both ordered a beer from the bar and sat there, side by side. After we clinked glasses to toast our friendship, Bert got down to business. "I have some work for you," he said.

I sat on the edge of my barstool and salivated in anticipation. "I want you to find Mr. MacGuffin," he said, as he sucked the suds off the head of his beer.

I was surprised at how let down I felt; I thought I had left all my dreams of Hollywood behind. What had I been anticipating, that Bert had another big studio movie job and wanted me to cowrite it with him? Still, a missing person case was nothing to sneeze at. So, I pulled open my notepad and asked, "When was the last time Mr. MacGuffin was seen?"

Bert scrunched his left eye shut to think and came back with, "The last confirmed sighting of Mr. MacGuffin was 1968, give or take."

I closed the notebook, not liking where this was heading. "1968? Don't you think Mr. MacGuffin would be long dead by now?"

*"...it had been a long time since I had seen him in the flesh.
He hadn't changed much. He must have been about fifty now,
and the only hint that he had aged since the last time I saw him
was some graying around the temples."*

"Oh, I should explain. Mr. MacGuffin isn't a person but a thing."

"A thing?"

"Well, to be clear, Mr. MacGuffin is an exact replica of Rudolph Valentino's erect penis made when the great actor was still alive. It was made of plaster of Paris and then painted purple."

I was beginning to think that I was about to be stiffed and, before the night was over, not only wouldn't I have any work out of this get-together, I would also end up picking up the bar tab.

"Look. I …" I began, before being stopped when Bert held up his hand to silence me.

"This isn't what you think. This is a very valuable piece of Hollywood memorabilia that is worth a small fortune."

"A valuable piece of Hollywood memorabilia?" I asked incredulously.

Bert nodded and asked, "You are aware of who Rudolph Valentino is, aren't you?"

"Of course," I sniffed, a little insulted that Bert would think I didn't know the first matinée movie star from the silent era, a man who could make women swoon from a glance and who died tragically young in the 1920s, breaking women's hearts all across the country.

"When it came to women, Valentino made Hugh Hefner look like an amateur. He had quality pussy hanging off of him anytime he wanted."

I should interject that Bert wasn't the type of guy who gave a hot damn about things like being politically correct or the #metoo movement. That and that alone may have been his only redeeming quality.

"Well, anyway, what's a guy to do? So many women, so little time, right? Only so much of him to go around. So, as a joke, one drunken weekend with his pals in Palm Springs, he had six of these erect penises, exact replicas of himself, made up. This way there would be more of him to go around. Get it?"

I didn't really and felt a little queasy as I took a sip from my draft, but I knew from experience not to interrupt Bert when he was on a roll.

"Now these replicas weren't a secret. As a laugh he actually named all six and would bring them to Hollywood parties. All of the show business community knew about them. They were so popular that, over time, he handed out the penises to friends as a thank you when they did a favor for him."

The bar door opened again, sending a chill our way, and we glanced toward the door before Bert continued. "Then Valentino dies and, as the years go by, all but one of these replicas disappear, presumably lost to history forever."

"And that takes us to 1968," I interjected.

"Exactly," said Bert, pointing a big meaty finger at me. "Did you ever hear of Pedro Noboa?"

"Can't say that I have."

"No surprise there," said Bert. "He was a minor character actor who did some early TV and was in some of those horrible B sci-fi movies that they used to make and show at drive-ins. He was known to have the last existing Valentino, the one named Mr. MacGuffin. He had inherited it several years earlier from an older actor he was friendly with when he died, who was one of Valentino's pals back in the day. Word was he kept this priceless piece of Hollywood kitsch on his desk and used it as a paperweight."

"A paperweight?"

Bert shrugged as if to say "to each his own."

"Anyway, Mr. Noboa was engaged to get married. In the summer of 1968, his fiancée hadn't heard from him in several days and was worried, so she convinced his landlord to open his apartment door and do a check on him. You know what he finds?"

I was about to guess, but Bert didn't have the patience to wait for my answer and said, "A dead body. And not just any dead body, mind you. Apparently, our friend, the character actor, was queer on the sly. They found him strangled to death, and he was all tied up with the usual B&D implements and had the words 'whip me' written on his ass.

"It didn't take Hollywood homicide long to bust the suspects. It turned out it was a couple of homo hustlers who were mad that Mr. Noboa didn't have the cash he promised them for his night of fun. Legend has it they took Mr. MacGuffin as a souvenir when they walked out the door after killing him. But when the police busted them, they either didn't care about Mr. MacGuffin or didn't know about it. The boys spent the rest of their lives in prison, and, according to rumor, Mr. MacGuffin then went from hand to hand, pardon the pun, disappearing for awhile only to resurface every now and again."

"Then I take it that it has resurfaced again?"

"Indeed it has, and I know who has it."

"I'm a little confused," I said. "I'm a detective, but it sounds like this isn't a mystery. What is it that I can do for you?"

"MacGuffin is right here in Baltimore," said Bert hardily. "I know I can trust you, and you have certain skills I'm sure you have acquired in your line of work that will be helpful in stealing it."

"Stealing it? Me?" I replied sharply. "No way am I getting involved in this, if it involves stealing."

Bert put his arm around my shoulder like we were old pals, saying, "Listen. What do you think is going to happen even if you're caught? The owner can't turn you in to the police, as this isn't his property. And even if he did, how much time do you think you would get for stealing a dildo that doesn't rightfully belong to anyone?"

Bert was probably right about that. With violent crime running rampant, Baltimore PD was satisfied if they could clear a homicide every now and again. Even if it did get reported, property theft wasn't exactly a high priority with Town Hall. Still, stealing was stealing. "I don't think I can help you," I said.

"You haven't heard the punch line," said Bert. "I have a guy in Hollywood who is willing to give me a half-million in cash for it. He's legit and loaded. I'll split it with you fifty-fifty if you acquire Mr. MacGuffin for me. I don't know about you, but I need a little cash to get my next project off the ground, and I'm guessing that amount of money might make a difference in your life."

I still should have said no, but by then we had switched to scotch and sodas, which must have clouded my judgment. I found myself hazily agreeing to Bert's scheme. Ah, firewater, the fuel of my introduction into criminality.

As we were walking out the door after calling it a night, I asked, "So who has MacGuffin now?"

"Have you ever heard of Cy Green?"

Indeed, I had, and the mere mention of his name scared the you-know-what out of me.

Chapter Two

The next afternoon in my office I allowed myself to think of Cy Green. I even Googled him to refresh my memory, although that wasn't really necessary. For twenty years, Cy Green had been the box office king of Hollywood, specializing as a director of horror flicks.

Just like his idol, Alfred Hitchcock, Green was obese and obscenely so, with most of his weight hanging off his belly. He had a shock of gray hair, parted on the side, that was so vibrant it screamed white instead of gray, which was in contrast to his beady brown eyes. But the most distinct feature of Green was his manner of speaking. He had a loud, commanding voice that made it seem like he was yelling even when he was speaking softly. His clipped, formal diction highlighted his perfect elocution and his flair for choosing the most apt word and pronunciation no matter the situation. When he spoke, you were reminded he was twice as smart as you, even on your best day.

In his heyday, Cy Green had ruled Hollywood with an iron fist. His ability to manufacture mass quantities of box-office bucks convinced the movie studios to look the other way and let him do as he pleased, and he used this carte blanche to be one of the worst bullies that Hollywood has ever seen. It didn't matter if you were an A-list actor, power agent, billionaire, or best boy, if you stepped on his set while he was filming you were his to abuse, and he did so at will.

He screwed whoever he wanted, reduced to tears anyone who challenged him, and even reportedly knocked a studio head out cold when he dared suggest a small edit.

All this had been pretty much an open secret. But he was so terrifying that even during the present age of the #metoo movement, not one person had publicly accused him of anything improper. You didn't fuck with Cy Green.

Five years ago, two weeks after the premier of his latest movie blockbuster, *High School Graduation Fright Night IV*, Cy stunned the world by announcing his retirement. He blamed his departure on how vapid Hollywood and the movie industry had become, and, even though he wasn't yet sixty, he stated that he wanted to go out while he was still on top.

True to his word, Cy packed his bags, sold his mansions and, for whatever reason, moved back to the city he grew up in, Baltimore. He hadn't necessarily become a recluse since cashing in his chips, but he did make it a point to keep a low profile once he returned to Charm City.

Just then a shadow projected itself across my desk, causing me to break from my Google search and look up from my laptop. "Greetings," said the familiar voice coming from just outside my door.

First, to end your speculation, my office looks better than you'd imagine. It's on St. Paul Street, which is a respectable address in a not-so-respectable city. It's one of those office suites where you share a receptionist and conference room with other businesses. From the outside it looks impressive, and if you call me on the phone during business hours it sounds like I have my own secretary. In reality it's all an illusion and a cheap one at that, as the rent was affordable even to a piker like me.

"Right on time," I said.

I've known Dan since first grade when we discovered we had the same birthday and became pals. Such are the ties that bind you in childhood. After graduation we lost touch, but a few months after my dad died, I ran into him at a party given by a mutual friend.

We found ourselves chatting up the same young Latina, a temptress with seductive brown eyes and a reputation of not so much dating men as devouring them. She answered to the nickname of La Petarda, or firecracker, which fit her perfectly. In the end, she left the party with another man, leaving Dan and I alone to reconnect as we lamented where we went wrong. Since then he has been helping me out on a freelance basis at the Trowbridge Detective Agency.

Dan is black, and I'm white, a fact that we never found the need to discuss. I don't know his opinion on Freddie Grey or the Reverend Al Sharpton, and he never asks if I hope Donald Trump is going to make America great again. We also don't talk about our personal lives, families, or religion. In some ways we are nothing more than strangers passing in the street, but in certain respects we are as tight as brothers.

"What do you have for me this time?" asked Dan, tall and lean with an old school Afro. He cocked his head waiting for the answer. I had a propensity to give Dan what one would call the dirty work, work from which he never shied away. For his efforts I paid him cash, under the table, of course. I also bought a pair of Orioles tickets each opening day and then treated him as my guest. Dan backed the Birds with a passion.

I told Dan about my meeting with Bert and the proposition we had agreed on. I didn't hold anything back including that this was worth $250,000 to me. Dan, if anything, was discrete. You could hold a gun to his head and he wouldn't rat you out. He, as well as I, knew the code of the Baltimore streets by heart: stitches are for snitches. In some cities this was hyperbole. In Baltimore, if you ended up with just the stitches you were lucky.

"So, you want me to help you steal some purple penis," Dan concluded nonjudgmentally.

I nodded and added, "I definitely need your help with this. What will it take?"

I expected him to ask for half, and I was prepared to counter with $75,000.

Instead he surprised me by saying, "One dollar."

"One dollar?" I asked incredulously.

Dan shrugged, adding, "One dollar and for me to become your business partner. You keep all the money from MacGuffin, but my share will be a stake in your detective agency. I'd say about thirty-three percent of the business would be appropriate."

"Are you sure?" I responded, sweeping my arms in a grand motion to point out that my office was barren. "Some months I barely cover my nut. You might be buying into a whole lot of nothing."

"I'll take my chances," he said. "We're worth betting on."

"Sold," I said, before he could change his mind. "Tell you what, I'll make it forty percent if you do a favor for me."

"Do tell."

"There's this guy," I said. "Maybe it's my imagination, but after Bert and I parted ways last night I felt like I was being tailed by him on the way home. I didn't think much of it, but on my way to the office this morning, I saw him again. I want to find out who this guy is, and what, if anything, he's up to."

"You gotta give me more than that. You have a description?"

I thought about this for a while. Although I could see him perfectly in my head, something about his appearance rang false. "Well, he wore an expensive tan trench coat that's seen better days. He was young, maybe late twenties, early thirties, and white with unkempt brown hair and a wild look in his eyes. My impression was that he was a homeless junkie or someone trying to make you think that he was a homeless junkie."

Dan pondered this for a moment, and I knew what he was thinking. This was a city full of homeless junkies. Finding this guy could be a needle in a haystack. "OK, consider it done," he concluded. "He is as good as found."

We both sat content for a moment before Dan asked, "So when do we steal that penis?"

"As soon as possible," I replied.

Chapter Three

A few days later, well after dark, Dan and I caught an Uber to one of the few tourist areas in Baltimore, the Inner Harbor. On the ride, Dan yakked on about the Orioles' offseason moves and how next year could be their year. When it came to the Orioles, Dan was an eternal optimist. But It was never going to be the Birds' year again. Call it the curse of Jim Palmer. Palmer was the only player active for all of the Orioles' three World Championships: 1966, 1970, and 1983. Since the pretty boy ace retired, however, baseball in Baltimore, for the most part, has been downright ugly.

At one point during the ride I almost interrupted Dan to tell him I had seen my stalker again yesterday, the guy with the crazy eyes, and this time I was positive he was tailing me. In the end I kept this information to myself. Dan, like most guys, didn't like being told how to do his job, and I knew him well enough to know that if he felt like I was putting pressure on him, he would resent it.

We told the driver to let us out at the National Aquarium. Our cover, if anyone questioned us, was that we were just a couple of guys out enjoying Baltimore's nightlife. The Inner Harbor was home to plenty of restaurants and bars that were hopping late into the night, so for us to be in the neighborhood would be perfectly reasonable.

Cy Green lived in a two-story penthouse in a swanky thirty-eight-story high-rise that overlooked the harbor and was Baltimore's hottest address. His condo was a half-mile walk from the Aquarium. After we got out of the Uber, we started the walk without talking.

The plan we had come up with for stealing Mr. MacGuffin was based on good fortune. After we figured out Cy's address, Dan realized he had a good buddy who worked security overnight in the building. Two years earlier this so-called buddy had asked Dan to pick up a package from a third party and hold it for him, as he was out of town for the weekend. Unbeknownst to Dan, the *package* turned out to contain a stolen smart phone. Thanks to the GPS chip, the owner of the phone, who just happened to be a local drug dealer, tracked Dan down and beat the shit out of him before taking his property back. Dan's friend owed him big for taking the beating, and to pay back the favor he had agreed to work with us on a plan to get us in and out of the building without getting caught. Only in Baltimore would a guy like this work in *security*.

When we got within a block of the high-rise Dan got out his cell and called his friend. "Randy, my man—we're here," he said. He ended the call abruptly and jutted his chin toward the building, saying "Let's go."

Inside the high-rise, the lobby was granite and marble with high-end finishes, and sitting at the concierge station was Dan's friend Randy in a security guard's blue blazer.

After brief introductions Randy said, "On the overnight I'm the only one here. Maintenance, housekeeping, and the security supervisor are only in during the day. If we have any alarms go off, they tend not to take it too seriously. It usually takes them about forty-five minutes to get in to respond."

As planned, Randy had killed the power to the CCTV equipment in the building when Dan had called him.

Without CCTV we could ransack the building with a cloak of invisibility. Cutting the power to the cameras would set off a silent alarm, but Randy assured us that if we were quick, we could be out of the building before anyone came in to restore the power to the cameras.

"Are you sure Mr. Green is out for the evening?" I asked.

"Positive. He lives alone, and I saw him last night getting into a limo. I asked him where he was going, and he told me he was going up to New York for a few days to pick up some film industry award."

I nodded, then said to Dan while looking at my watch, "Let's get moving. If we only have forty-five minutes, let's try to do it in thirty."

Cy Green was the only resident on the top two floors of the building, and he and he alone had a swipe card that allowed him up to the penthouse in the elevator. The building did have an internal stairwell that residents could use as an exit in case of a fire. The door was locked on the lobby level to prevent unwanted people from accessing it. Security held a master key for it, and Randy left his concierge post and unlocked the stairwell. "All the way to thirty-eight," he said as he held the door open for us. When the door shut behind us, we could hear him yell, "You won't need a key to get back into the stairwell to go down."

Dan and I started up the stairs at a brisk jog, which within a few flights turned into a hearty walk, and by the time we'd gotten to the last few flights, we were crawling up the stairwell clinging to the bannister. It had taken over fifteen minutes to make it all the way up, but we reasoned that the trip back down would go faster. Still, there wasn't much time.

The door to Cy Green's multimillion-dollar pad was plain and simple. "OK, partner, do your thing," I said to Dan, encouraging him to break down the door.

Dan stood hunched over with his hands on his knees, and between gulping breaths said, "You gotta be kidding me. I barely have enough energy to stand."

Fortunately, I was kidding him. I had been carrying a shopping bag from Kohl's that I thought would look inconspicuous if I was seen toting it around. I had shoved the bag full of packing peanuts and some bubble wrap to keep MacGuffin safe from breakage after we stole it. Digging around to the bottom of the bag I found what I wanted, and produced the leather case containing several lock picks. I didn't know one small-time detective who was worth a damn who didn't have their own picks and know how to use them.

Green had double-locks. The first lock yielded in seconds. The second took me a good three minutes and several picks before I heard that familiar click. "We're in," I said to Dan triumphantly. I looked at my watch and guessed we had about seventeen minutes left.

It was pitch dark when we entered the apartment. I fumbled for a wall switch and found one that flooded the place with light.

"Wow," said Dan.

Wow, indeed. The penthouse had floor-to-ceiling glass windows with views of both the harbor and downtown. From this vantage point, even Baltimore looked beautiful. "Come on," I said. "We don't have time to sightsee. We have to find MacGuffin."

With two large floors to cover I was worried we wouldn't have enough time, but I scanned the room carefully. It looked like a palatial living room with trendy modern furniture that I couldn't picture the oversized Cy Green being comfortable sitting in. In the center of the room was an ornate spiral staircase that led down to the lower floor. The place was huge. MacGuffin could be anywhere.

I scrutinized the walls and saw plenty of artwork that I assumed were originals and worth a fortune. Oddly, I didn't see any photos of Green or personal items on display, nor any movie posters or anything else that would demonstrate to a visitor that not too long ago, Cy Green had been the King of Hollywood.

Then a glass case caught my eye, and I walked over to it. "Well, well," I said. "This is going to be easier than I thought."

"What do you have?" asked Dan, coming up behind me.

Inside the case, which butted up against the wall, there was a podium at eye level with a purple penis on it. The case was constructed of thick glass. At the bottom of the podium was an inscription on a silver plate that I read out loud: "Rudolph Valentino 1895–1926."

I studied the glass carefully for a few minutes, trying to see if it had an alarm and considering options for ways that we could get MacGuffin out without getting caught. While thinking this over, I sensed that Dan had walked back over to where I was. I felt a sudden whoosh of air and then heard the sound of crashing glass. While I had been contemplating, Dan had gone into the kitchen, grabbed a metal pot, and had simply smashed the glass.

The loud sound of the breaking glass was startling, but after a moment it was quiet and no audible alarm had gone off. I grabbed MacGuffin from the podium and examined it. I noticed that it must have been behind glass for a while, because it was dusty. Holding it in my hand, I gave it a few quick blows to clean it off.

Over my shoulder I could feel Dan staring at me. I quickly pulled some bubble wrap from my Kohl's bag to encase it in,

"I felt a sudden whoosh of air and then heard the sound of crashing glass. While I had been contemplating, Dan had gone into the kitchen, grabbed a metal pot, and had simply smashed the glass."

then gently dropped it into the bag, making sure the packing peanuts nestled it securely. I looked at my watch. "We only have about seven minutes left. We have to get out of here."

Dan headed back toward the stairwell, but I yelled, "We don't have time to walk down. We'll have to risk it." I nodded my head to the elevator, pushing the down button. The elevator arrived quickly with a ding, and we started down as soon as I hit the button to the lobby.

Then something happened that hadn't been accounted for in our plan. When we got to the seventeenth floor the elevator stopped and a woman got on. And not just any woman at that, but a honey blonde with high cheekbones wearing a tight red dress and formal gold pumps. She was, simply put, to die for.

She seemed surprised to see us, but recovered quickly and said, "Good evening," as she entered. She had a slight English accent, and for some reason my heart always melts for women with English accents.

Being the gentlemen that we are, Dan and I backed up to allow her space to get on, which she did. When she turned to face the front of the elevator, I noted she looked as good from the back as she did from the front.

All of this should be just trivia, but when we got between the eighth and seventh floors the elevator came to a shuttering stop, and I flew forward so hard that I practically knocked this beauty over; I had to hold her up to prevent her from falling.

In the now-stuck elevator she turned to me with a smile and said, "Well, I have to give you credit. Most men aren't as creative as you when they try to grope me." Ah, a woman with a sense of humor and personality—I like that.

I should stop right now and explain something. Women, or at least certain types of women, find me attractive. I have broad shoulders, dimples, and what I have been told by one of my ex-girlfriends are dark brown hypnotic eyes. This chance encounter had serious potential.

For the next few minutes while we were stuck, we shamelessly flirted. Her name was Natalie. She was dressed up to go to a party that she said she would rather not be going to, and she had a wide beautiful smile that showed off perfect teeth when she laughed.

In the background, I could see Dan looking uncomfortable. As every second ticked by it was becoming more likely maintenance would arrive and restore power to the CCTV, and our images would be captured. If Cy Green chose to report this theft to the police we were cooked. While Dan sweated over this fact, I was having too much fun in the moment to care.

But then the elevator stuttered to life again. I tumbled into Natalie once more, and we both laughed. When we made it to the lobby, I asked for her phone number and offered to buy her dinner one night. She obliged with her number, but said, "I don't know if you have to waste money on dinner with me, since we've already achieved physical intimacy. Let's go out for some drinks and skip the pretense." Drinks it was.

Just before she walked out the front door, Natalie turned to me and said, "How will I know it's you when you call? I didn't catch your name."

"The last name is Trowbridge. First name is Phillip, but only my mother has called me that," I said. "Friends just call me Trow."

"OK, Trow," she replied. "I'll be expecting that call." Then she slipped into the night.

Randy at the concierge desk gave us a quick thumbs up, letting us know that the CCTV cameras weren't back on yet. We thanked him and he said to me, "I see you met Natalie Green."

I didn't make the connection at first, but Dan caught on quickly. "This Natalie Green. She wouldn't be related to Cy Green, would she?" he asked.

"Of course. She's his daughter."

We walked back to the Aquarium in silence, me toting my Kohl's shopping bag with Mr. MacGuffin and my picks in it. I ordered an Uber to get home, the modern getaway car for our times. As the Uber pulled up, Dan finally broke his silence saying. "You do know that girl is bad news, don't you?"

Chapter Four

Bert picked up on the third ring. "I got it," I said.

"You got it?"

"I got it!"

"Is it authentic?" he asked.

"How would I know?" I asked.

It was midnight, and I was back in my office alone after sending Dan home for the night. Pushing the packing peanuts aside, I pulled Mr. MacGuffin out of my Kohl's shopping bag and unwrapped it from the bubble wrap. I held it up, spinning it around and taking a good long look at it for the first time. "Well, I don't see any made in China stamps on it, so I take that as a good sign."

"Describe it to me."

"Describe it to you?"

"Yes, describe it to me. Take a look at it and tell me what you see."

"Well, it's purple," I said.

"How purple?"

"How purple?" I repeated quizzically. I took another look and answered my own question. "A light purple," I said. "It looks like it was darker originally and has faded over the years. If I had to describe the color now, I would use the term mauve," I said, impressed by my own vocabulary.

"Now describe the object itself."

I had to think about how best to put this. Mr. MacGuffin was remarkably detailed, with veins and the head clearly depicted. "It looks like a very thorough replication of the male unit."

"Tell me about the size," asked Bert.

"It appears to be perfectly average in length and width." I couldn't help but do a mental comparison to myself and wondered if Valentino was tempted to add an inch or two to satisfy his male ego during that drunken weekend in Palm Springs.

Bert was quiet on his end of the line, and I didn't know if I lost him, so I quipped, "Valentino looks to have been a perfectly healthy male, but certainly no Milton Berle."

"Trow, my boy, you've done it. You've done it! You have the original Mr. MacGuffin." I had known Bert for years, and I don't recall ever hearing him happier.

"So, what do we do now?" I asked. "Do you want me to put it in a box and ship it to you UPS Priority?"

"What?" he yelled. "Are you crazy?" "This is a priceless piece of Americana. If you had the *Mona Lisa*, would you slip it in a FedEx package and send it that way?"

"So, what do you want me to do with it?"

"Nothing," he replied. "I'll make arrangements to fly in from LA and pick it up in person. In the meantime, keep a low profile and guard it with your life." I didn't have the heart to tell him neither of those things was going to happen, and we hung up amicably with Bert still over the moon about Mr. MacGuffin being in my possession.

The next day I got another cryptic email from Bert that made no mention of the stolen object, only that the following morning he was catching a flight from LA to Baltimore and he wanted to see me again in the same location we had met last week.

As a precaution, I secured MacGuffin in a safe-deposit box I had, so I wouldn't have to babysit the damn thing until Bert returned. I then made a date with Natalie Green for that night.

I know what you're thinking. Dan was right: this is bad news and I should be staying as far away from Cy Green's daughter as possible. But I had to admit I was hooked and had been since the moment I fell into her on the elevator.

We agreed to meet for dinner instead of drinks because, after all, that was the gallant thing to do. She suggested a new restaurant in Fells Point, which boasted a celebrity chef who had a James Beard Award and his own cable TV show. I checked out their website and realized this date was going to hurt my wallet, but I bet on Natalie Green being worth the investment.

I got there first, and was seated at a table in the ultra-modern interior of the restaurant. I realized it was one of those places where you paid for waiters who explained every detail of the dish you ordered, and for chefs who took great pride in drizzling the bottom of the plate, as if it were artwork.

Five minutes after our scheduled date time, Natalie made a spectacular entrance. She was wearing a different red dress than the one I had seen her in last, this one less snug, but with a scoop neck showing cleavage. She caught my eye and flashed a smile, and I was taken again by how beautiful she was and rose in respect as she came to the table.

Our date got off to a bit of a rough start when she said sharply, "I think you may have an ulterior motive in trying to get on my good side."

Every straight man on a date with a beautiful woman has an ulterior motive, but I didn't think this would be a polite way to respond; instead, I innocently asked, "What do you mean?"

"I've done a little Internet research on you this afternoon and see you used to be a writer. Are you using me to get to my father, Cy Green, the famous director, in hopes he'll look at a script you're working on?"

I laughed and told a small white lie, saying "Until now I didn't realize there was a connection between you and Cy." Then I spilled the whole story of how I ended up in Hollywood, how I bottomed out in show business, my drunken dad, and how I was now quite content running a detective agency.

In all, she was sympathetic to my sad tale, which made me feel like a million bucks. Now it was her turn to talk, and for the rest of dinner she reciprocated by telling me her life story. Cy, as Natalie called him, never once referring to him as "dad" or "father," was apparently as awful in his personal life as he was on the movie set.

Natalie's mother had been a young, aspiring English actress who Cy had romanced with beautiful words and promises of movie parts, which all ended when she became pregnant with Natalie. Not only did the movie parts not come, but he shipped her back to England with a small stipend of cash and threats that she not contact him again or dare to get back into show business.

Cy even went so far as denying he was Natalie's father until she was a teenager, when her mother, finally showing some backbone, threatened to take him to court unless he publicly acknowledged her paternity Even after that connection was established, contact between Natalie and Cy was sporadic: a phone call on her birthday, lunch if he was in London on business. Cy did take financial responsibility, sending her to the best schools in England and giving her a generous allowance as an adult.

"I don't think he means to be so horrible," she said. "It's just that he is obsessive. If he wants something, he's relentless until he gets it and everything else in the world will take a back seat. That is what made him such a great film director. There were no distractions allowed, including things like wives and children. For him, it was always making his next film as perfect as possible."

I squirmed in my seat and wondered: Now that I had stolen Mr. MacGuffin from him, would his new obsession be to get it back? And to what lengths would he go? Instead of pursuing this train of thoughts, I changed the subject slightly and asked, "If he liked making movies so much, why did he walk away from the business?"

"Don't believe that nonsense that he wanted to leave while still on top of his game. Cy is never off the top of his game. The real reason is his health. Between his work schedule, his weight, and the pressure of making movies over the years, his heart is shot. His doctor told him that if he kept making movies, he would be dead sooner rather than later.

"When he moved back to Baltimore, he begged me to get involved in his life, to reconnect with him, and to keep an eye on him so he wasn't drawn back into the business. At the time I was living in Manhattan and doing well as the owner and editor of a web magazine dedicated to interior design. The last thing I wanted was to give up my life to keep an eye on Cy Green."

"So, what changed your mind?"

Natalie looked at me sheepishly and said, "Just like the *Godfather*, he made me an offer I couldn't refuse. He bought me the whole seventeenth floor in the building where we met as a down payment, and now he pays me an obscene monthly salary to be his *personal assistant*," she said, rolling her eyes. "In the end I agreed, as long as the duties left me enough time to keep working on my magazine."

One thing about Natalie was that the more she talked, the more the rest of the world faded away. She was smart, witty, sexy, and surprisingly well-grounded. I couldn't remember the food being brought to the table, or our eating it, or any of the background noise in the restaurant. All I know is that at one point we finished dinner and the check arrived.

After the meal she offered me the opportunity to go back to her place. She had just finished building a personal movie theater that she was proud of and wanted to show it off. I agreed to go back and watch a movie with her as long as it wasn't one of Cy's horror flicks. She laughed and agreed.

In the morning, leaving her place, I felt like a new and improved man. That Trowbridge fellow with a flawed life was no more; I was reborn and nothing was going to trip me up again. That feeling lasted only until I hit the lobby, and I noticed the lobby concierge in tears. The blue-vested concierge was on the phone. I overheard him say, "I'm sorry, Mr. Green. It will never happen again. I don't know how that FedEx package I signed on your behalf became damaged. I promise to pay any restitution."

I couldn't exactly make out what Cy said back but could clearly hear him roaring his disgust on the other end of the phone, yelling at the stunned concierge. I kept my head down and got out of the lobby as quickly as possible. My day was coming with Cy, I could feel it. Whatever confidence I had built up for that encounter had just drained away.

Chapter Five

I had just wrapped up a morning meeting with a potential client and was pondering what to tackle next. The husband of the woman who wanted to hire me had died six months ago, and she swore he had squirreled away more than $200,000 in various international bank accounts to keep it secret from the IRS. The only problem was, he had done such a good job of hiding the money that now he was dead, she couldn't find the loot either.

The client had offered to give me ten percent of the money I recovered. I turned her down. First, it sounded like a job more in the wheelhouse of a detective firm that specialized in cyber detection. Second, I rarely work on commission; commission left too much of a possibility of my investing a whole lot of time for a whole lot of nothing.

My contemplation was disrupted by a ruckus in the outer office. I got to my feet to see what the was going on just as Dan forcefully dragged a guy in through the office door by the nape of his neck. The man was protesting loudly to be let go.

"Is this the guy you've been looking for?" Dan asked, pulling the guy's head up by the collar while still gripping him firmly. I took a look, and sure enough, it was the same creepy guy with the wild eyes and expensive trench coat that needed a trip to the dry cleaners.

"That's the guy," I said.

"Grab a seat," said Dan as he roughly pushed him into a chair.

I reached out and shook Dan's hand saying, "Nice job, partner. It looks like you're up to forty percent now."

I took a good look at Wild Eyes. Up close he looked younger than I thought, and he was nervous as hell. The wild eyes weren't because he was crazy or high, just scared. "OK," I said. "What's your name?"

"I don't have to tell you anything."

I didn't have time for games so I reached into the breast pocket of his jacket without asking and pulled out his wallet. "Hey," he squealed in protest.

"Let's see what we have here," I said in a mocking tone. I pulled out his driver's license. "Well, well. Your name is Evan Andrews, and you have a Virginia driver's license with an address in McLean." I looked him in the eyes and said in a drawn-out drawl, "Fancy."

Rifling through his wallet some more I found a family photo of him with his young wife, holding a baby boy. "You got a beautiful family," I said, showing the picture to Dan.

"Give that back," he said protesting, starting to get out of his seat.

"Shut up and sit back down," replied Dan as he shoved him back into the chair.

After combing through the guy's wallet some more, I said to Dan, "Well, lookie here. It seems as though Mr. Andrews is a licensed detective in DC. If his business card is accurate, he works for one of the big, high-dollar firms that has a well-known reputation for working for all the elected crooks on Capitol Hill. Now," I said, turning to Andrews, "save us all some time and tell me who hired you to tail me."

The kid looked for a second, like he might cry at the harsh way we were handling him. Then he showed a little backbone by stiffening up and saying with as much resolve as he could muster, "I'll never divulge the name of our clients. Never."

For a second I almost respected him for that, but not quite. At this point Dan chimed in, asking, "How about bumping me up to fifty percent if I get the name out of him?"

Thinking that another ten percent of my beaten down detective agency wasn't much to give up, I said, "Go for it."

With a sadistic smile Dan sang out gleefully. "Can I borrow your lock picks?"

"Sure, what are you going to do with those?"

Matter-of-factly Dan replied, "Slowly remove each of his teeth until he talks. I bet he spills the beans before I get the third one out."

Andrews looked at him coldly and said, "You don't scare me."

I pulled Andrews' head back, and Dan began to work on his teeth after forcing the picks in his mouth. Within a minute I heard a crack, and Dan shot me a surprised look that conveyed, "Whoops. I didn't mean to do that. I was just trying to scare him."

I whispered to Dan, "You're back down to a thirty-three percent share."

Andrews cried out in pain, "OK. OK. Stop! I'll talk. Just don't hurt me anymore."

"OK, Mr. Andrews. Who hired you to tail me?"

His wild eyes were back and in a trembling voice he spit out, along with a gob of blood, "That director, Cy Green."

His answer threw me for a loop, but I tried to maintain my composure and asked, "Why?"

"First, I was hired to follow a Mr. Bert Thompson while he was in town from Los Angeles, to see what he was doing in Baltimore. I followed him for a whole day and Mr. Thompson did nothing noteworthy, but he met you for drinks, so afterward I started following you, believing you might be the reason why he was in the area. Once I figured out that you're a PI, I assumed that meant he must have hired you, so I decided to take the initiative and follow you to see if I could figure out what he hired you for."

"For your information," I said, "Bert and I are friends from way back when we were partners in another line of work. He didn't hire me. We were just two old friends catching up. Got it?"

"Got it," he said.

"Just curious. Why did Cy Green hire your firm to follow Bert Thompson?"

Andrews shrugged and said, "Don't know. I just know he wanted him followed, and he wanted a minute-by-minute update on what he did while he was in Baltimore."

I was out of questions, and Dan asked me, "So what do you want me to do with him now?"

"Like any small fish," I said, "throw him back. He's not worth the effort to scale and cook."

Dan led Andrews out of my office, where I'm sure he would hit the pavement with a tumble. I couldn't help but think of Cy Green; I figured the worst with him was going to come and come at any moment.

Before meeting Bert that night, I opened my safety-deposit box and retrieved Mr. MacGuffin, wrapping him up and shoving him into my now well-worn Kohl's shopping bag. Carrying around MacGuffin, I was starting to get paranoid, which caused me to look over my shoulder several times to make sure Mr. Wild Eyes or Cy Green weren't closing in on me from behind. I didn't have the stomach for being a thief, and I would be happy to pass on the merchandise and be done with this caper.

I arrived at the watering hole right on time and saw Bert had beaten me there. He had a corner of the bar to himself, with an empty stool next to him. He saw me and shouted, "Over here!"

Bert had a draft waiting for me, and was halfway into one of his own when I sat down next to him. For the next twenty minutes he complained about his flight and how the airline industry had gone to the dogs. When he started in on how bad the weather is in Baltimore compared to L.A., I had to put my foot down.

"Are we going to do this or what?" I asked, while reaching into my Kohl's bag.

Bert swiftly smacked my hand away from the bag whispering, "Are you crazy? We can't do this in here."

"So, where do you suggest we go?"

"Follow me," Bert said with a wave of his hand as he got off his barstool. I took a last big slug of my draft before following. It had been paid for, and I wasn't going to let it go to waste.

He led me to an alley next to the bar. It was dark and creepy and smelled of a mix of urine and garbage. If a rat the size of a fox had scurried past, I wouldn't have been surprised.

"OK, let's see it," he said.

I pulled MacGuffin out and held it up for Bert to inspect. He put on a pair of reading glasses then took out his cell phone and used the flashlight feature to inspect the artefact inch by inch. This went on for a good ten minutes as I watched in silence. Even though it was a cool evening, I could feel sweat beading on my forehead.

Finally, he put his glasses and phone away and said joyously, "I'm convinced that this is one hundred percent authentic, and we have the real MacGuffin."

Before I could respond he added, "Isn't it beautiful?"

"I'm not sure that is how I would describe it," I said, before putting MacGuffin back in my Kohl's bag.

"Trow, you did a terrific job, and you will be rewarded handsomely for your work. I'll take it now."

"Wait a second," I protested. "Where's the money? We have a deal. You get Mr. MacGuffin and I get $250,000 in cash."

"The money is in Baltimore," Bert promised earnestly. "The person who is buying it flew into town with me. He is in a hotel right now awaiting delivery. I give him MacGuffin, he gives me the cash. Then I give you your split."

"OK. Let's go meet him and give it to him right now," I replied.

"Uh, that is going to be a problem," said Bert slowly.

"And why is that?"

"Let me remind you we are in possession of stolen merchandise worth at least a half a million dollars. My client wants to deal only with me, and to keep as low of a profile as possible. I'm sure you understand that."

I did, but that didn't help my pocketbook any. I trusted Bert, but a quarter of a million dollars can even make old friends do squirrely things.

After a few more minutes of negotiating, I handed over the bag with MacGuffin in it, and Bert promised to meet me the next night at our meeting spot for the cash exchange.

I know what you're thinking at this point. I was a sucker for handing it over without getting the dough on the spot. But here's the thing. In a way I was relieved that I was handing over MacGuffin and would never see it again. Who knows, maybe not having it would keep Cy Green from tracking me down with the goon squad and working me over. Besides, I knew Bert well. He was a Hollywood guy and would never leave the area. If he split without giving me my cut, I could track him down in no time.

As he was walking away with my Kohl's bag, I gave Bert a warning. "Hey, just to give you a heads up, I learned today Cy Green is tailing you."

"Yeah? Who gives a shit? I mean what is he going to do? He can't exactly report me to the police. Besides, the guy who is buying this from me isn't exactly scared of Cy. If Cy has a problem with me, he can take it up with him."

Chapter Six

I should have been tense as I idled away the day while awaiting my rendezvous with Bert that evening, wondering if he would show with the cash. Instead, Natalie called and threw me a life preserver saying, "What do you say we get together?"

The weather had turned unexpectedly bright and warm, and we decided to celebrate this good fortune with a walk at the Inner Harbor. Baltimore was notoriously hot and muggy in the summer and cold and windy in the winter, the worst of both worlds. To let a rare perfect day go by without getting outside would have been a sin.

Natalie wore snug blue jeans and a light black sweater. It was the first time I had been with her that she wasn't dressed to kill and wearing red. Even when she downplayed it, Natalie stood out from the pack. Her honey-blond hair shimmered in the sunlight, and the dark shades she donned could easily fool passersby into thinking she was a famous actress trying to keep a low profile. People noticed us as we walked by as a couple, or at least they noticed Natalie. She looked like a million bucks.

We were both in rare moods and our conversation was easy and light. The Inner Harbor was busy with tourists and school groups taking in the sights. After getting jostled one time too many by the bustle, we naturally began holding hands so as not to get separated. We must have looked like a pair of dopey teenagers in love, and I kind of have to admit that is how I was feeling.

I treated us to some soft-serve ice cream, and we found an empty bench that had a nice view of the water. We were silent as we ate, and when Natalie spoke again her mood had turned dark.

"Cy is driving me mad."

"Oh?"

"He's impossible to deal with even on a good day, but ever since he returned from New York he has gone off the chain. If this keeps up, nice condo and hefty salary or not, I'm going to tell him to shove it and go back to life without a father." Natalie was so worked up her high cheekbones had darkened to a mix between rose and blush.

Now I had a sinking feeling in my stomach, but being a detective, I felt the need to push for specifics. "What's gotten him so worked up?"

"Who knows?" she replied dismissively. "I have my theory, but when I asked I was told it was none of my business. That would be fine by me, except that he keeps making it my business by cussing like a sailor and ranting that he is going to 'get those sons of bitches no matter what it costs' and 'no matter how many rocks he has to turn over.' I told you he is obsessive when he gets onto something. Well, this is his thing at the moment, and it is driving me mad."

It was fair for me at this juncture to wonder what Natalie really knew. After all, she had probably been in Cy's place countless times, and MacGuffin had been displayed in plain sight in his living room. What could a classy woman like Natalie have thought of such a crude phallic symbol being a prized possession of her father? Did she view it as a harmless Hollywood memento from one of the silent era's biggest stars, or did she see it as sick and perverted, something that objectified women by paying homage to male sexuality?

I also assumed that she had been in Cy's place since it had been stolen and would probably have noticed this by now. Had she put two and two together, understanding that this was what was drawing her father's ire, but being too polite to bring up such a gross subject to a new boyfriend? Troubling me further was the fact that it would probably only be a matter of time before she would ask me what Dan and I had been doing in her building that night we met.

All of these thoughts played on in me, but as she talked all I could do was to be was sympathetic and hope that she changed the subject. Eventually she did, saying, "You're very sweet to listen to me go on."

I told her it wasn't a bother, and she asked if we could get together that night. I couldn't, of course, as I had my meeting with Bert. She looked disappointed when I told her I had to work. However, I quickly got a rain check for the following day, and her face and my mood brightened.

* * * * *

I arrived ten minutes early for the meeting with Bert and ordered a rum and Coke to kill the time until he joined me. The rum settled my nerves, and it was a nice change from the draft beer that was flat and listless in this place.

After a good half-hour and another rum and Coke, it sunk in that Bert wasn't going to show. I felt stupid for being so trusting and chided myself for falling for the "I'll pay you later" gambit, the oldest bit in the book. But then I had a thought. What had Bert really said last night, something about meeting in the same spot tomorrow night? When Bert had set up the meeting for tonight, he and I were in the alley right next to the bar. It was a long shot and it didn't really make sense, but what if Bert has been waiting for me in the alley with my cash?

I flipped a ten spot at the bartender and didn't wait for change but headed straight to the alley. Looking down the alley I didn't see anything, which didn't mean a whole heck of a lot, as it was dark. "Bert?" I called out.

As soon as I said this, I heard some movement in the alley. My instincts kicked in and without knowing who was down there I started running toward where I heard the noise. Now the sound of someone running away was unmistakable, and it was clear that whoever I'd heard was heading further back into the alley. I prided myself in being fast and assumed I was making up ground with each step. Just then, however, I tripped over something large and soft and did a face plant right into the pavement.

I got up and did a quick inventory to see if I was hurt and then marshaled on. The alley came to an abrupt end a few feet away, where there was a five-foot chain-link fence. Whoever had been in the alley with me had clearly climbed over the fence and was too far gone for me to follow.

A chill came over me that had nothing to do with the night air. What was it that had I fallen over? Was my short-term memory playing tricks on me or did I really hear a jingle when I tripped? Then I thought of my old writing partner's necklaces and chains and shouted to no one, "Bert, damn it! What have you gotten us into?"

I slowly retraced my steps until I came upon a mass midway down the alley. It was too dark to see anything, so I crouched down, pulled out my phone, and flipped on the flashlight feature. "Bert?" I whispered softly, but there was no reply.

Although Bert's body was still warm, I couldn't pick up a pulse. Without touching his body any more than I had to and running the flashlight over the length of him, it didn't take a CSI to tell me that Bert had died from a single gunshot to the temple.

I was now in a major jam, and there was no way I could call this crime into the police without becoming the prime suspect myself and possibly getting arrested for a major theft at the same time. The best I could do now was stall for time and try to piece together what happened as quickly as possible. Deftly I pulled out Bert's wallet and grabbed his cell phone. Once the police IDed the cadaver as Bert Thompson, it wouldn't take them long to connect the dots to me. Taking the items that easily identified Bert would buy me some extra time. And with all the homicides stacking up in Baltimore, it might take a while before the police had the time to even figure out who they had lying in the morgue.

Before leaving the alley, I looked both ways to make sure the coast was clear and got the hell out of there.

Chapter Seven

At midnight, back at my brownstone in Pigstown, I had coffee brewing and was debriefing Dan on the events of the night, including the facts that both Mr. MacGuffin and the cash were nowhere to be found.

I had called Dan as soon as I arrived home. When he answered, he seemed to sense a problem, asking, "What's wrong?" When I said "Plenty," but couldn't talk over the phone, he said he'd be right over.

Dan had always liked my brownstone in Pigstown. I guess that's because it's near Oriole Park and when the Orioles are playing at night you can see the stadium lights from my stoop. That may sound romantic if you're a baseball fan, but on game nights people attending the games spill over into our neighborhood to park, often leaving the residents to scramble to find a spot of their own. One night of having to park your car several blocks away from your home will jade you pretty quickly.

"So, you think your buddy Bert was waiting for you in an alley with a quarter of a million and got mugged by chance?"

I pictured that scenario. Some lowlife thief rolls Bert and kills him, thinking he's getting, what, some pocket change in a satchel Bert is carrying only to find to his surprise when he opens the satchel that he has $250,000? Talk about hitting the jackpot.

"Maybe. Maybe not," I replied. "Another scenario is the guy who was supposed to exchange the money for the MacGuffin double-crossed Bert and killed him, keeping both the MacGuffin and the cash for himself, a real win-win for the mystery buyer that Bert brought with him from Hollywood."

Dan had connections with the Baltimore Police, and we had already discussed how he would try to monitor what they knew and when. Have they found the body, did they have any CCTV footage of the area, and had they IDed Bert and made the connection to me yet? Getting inside information on all of this would help me know how I could best maneuver.

Our conversation was interrupted by a clear, crisp bell tone from my door. I felt my heart jump and said, "Crap, I can't believe it. The police are on to me already."

Dan, who was peering out the corner of my blinds by my bay window, said, "That looks like no cop I've ever seen."

I walked over to Dan and snuck a peek myself. Standing on my stoop was a young white guy with wavy brown hair in serious need of a comb. He stood about five foot nothing and by the porchlight I could see that he was wearing an expensive looking Italian suit and what looked like authentic Berluti leather Oxford shoes. The outfit was impractical for a homicide detective to wear, and the shoes alone could get you killed wearing them in Baltimore.

Impatiently, the man pushed my doorbell again as he stamped his feet nervously on my stoop. Brownstone stoops have a long history in Baltimore; not that long ago the residents, despite whatever else they had going on in their lives, would wash the steps of their stoops by hand to always make sure they were bright and white. It was an unwritten competition among neighbors, each trying to outdo the other. Those days were gone, and my generation was satisfied with our stoops as long as we didn't see fresh blood on them in the morning when we went out.

"Hold your horses," I shouted. I motioned for Dan to hide in the kitchen in case this guy came in and tried to get the drop on me. If that happened Dan could repay the favor.

I opened the door saying, "I don't want any," rather curtly.

"MacGuffin. I demand Mr. MacGuffin," he shouted. I didn't need my neighbors overhearing this potentially incriminating information while Bert Thompson's body was cooling across town, so I quickly invited my late-night visitor inside my brownstone.

Inside, the visitor calmed down and took stock of his surroundings, all the while with a disapproving expression on his face. It was obvious he wasn't a fan of my interior decorating skills, which, I had to admit, were influenced more by comfort and economy rather than by a cohesive style or aesthetic.

"Just who are you, and what are you doing at my house this late at night?" I asked, trying to sound menacing.

"My name is Peter Laverany, and I made a deal with your friend, Bert Thompson. I offered to pay him a million dollars for Mr. MacGuffin. I know he is a business associate of yours, as he told me you stole MacGuffin for him. Tonight, he was scheduled to come to my hotel and make the exchange. He didn't show up, and now I need to find him. We had a deal. Mr. MacGuffin is rightfully mine. If Mr. Thompson won't fulfill our deal, I'm willing to pay you the million if you have it."

Laverany had an accent I couldn't quite place. Was it South American? Eastern European? Or was it from some other exotic locale? I figured that he was more than likely gay, as the slight lilt in his voice was setting off even my not-too-finely-tuned gaydar. You won't get noticed speaking that way in Hollywood, but in Pigstown you stand out like a sore thumb.

"Listen, pal," I said as kindly as I could. "I don't have Mr. MacGuffin, and Bert Thompson right about now is probably landing on a slab in the city morgue. If you're smart, you'll get on the first plane back to L.A. in the morning and forget all about Mr. MacGuffin."

Hearing about Bert Thompson's death didn't faze my relentless guest, who for the next hour must have gone through six cigarettes, lighting up each without asking my permission and vowing not to leave Baltimore without having what he came for. Before he finally left, he handed me a card with his cell phone number on it and told me if I had MacGuffin or could find it, *he would now pay me up to two million for it.*

When he left, I turned to Dan and said, "The nerve of that guy."

"The nerve of your so-called friend Bert Thompson," Dan fired back. "It sounds like he was going to get a million for MacGuffin, and your fifty-percent cut only amounted to $250,000. My Baltimore schooling may not be the best, but that's no fifty percent. Your old writing partner was going to rip you off."

"I wonder who else he ripped off?" I asked. "And I wonder if whoever else he ripped off didn't take it very well in the alley tonight?"

Chapter Eight

The next day Dan stopped by my office to give me an update on what he had heard from his connection in the Baltimore PD. "First, the bad news," he said matter-of-factly. "Around ten this morning someone noticed Bert Thompson in the alley and reported it to the police."

"And the good news?" I asked.

"They have no CCTV footage from the alley or nearby, and they still haven't IDed Bert yet. Best of all," said Dan with a sly smile, "Baltimore is dealing with a higher profile homicide today since one of the mayor's friends was whacked in a liquor store a few hours ago. It was a robbery that went bad, and the mayor's friend was just a poor schmuck customer who was in the wrong place at the wrong time. As you can imagine, Baltimore PD is running around frantically trying to catch the perp 'cause the mayor is breathing down the police commissioner's neck."

"Hopefully, this buys me enough time to straighten all this out first," I said.

"Straighten it all out? And just how are you going to do that?"

"I'm working on a plan right now," I said.

What I didn't tell Dan is that I had absolutely no plan, and without a plan there was not much I could do except hope for police incompetence till I could figure out how to save my bacon.

That evening I had a date with Natalie and left work early to shave and shower. The place she suggested was just a block from her waterfront condo and when I got there I was relieved to see it was a simple burger-and-fries joint. Although she was worth it, tonight's date was more in line with my budget than the five-star eatery we had gone to previously.

I got there first and grabbed a table. A perky waitress named Molly dropped off a pair of menus after I said I was expecting a guest. Five minutes later Molly reappeared, asking, "Are you Mr. Trowbridge?"

"Yes," I said, puzzled that she knew my name.

"We just received a call from a Miss Natalie Green saying she was running about twenty minutes late. She is sending her apologies and asked that I deliver this to help pass the time." With that she handed me a draft off the tray she was carrying.

I thanked her and took a healthy slurp and pondered my next move regarding MacGuffin. Earlier that day I had Googled Peter Laverany and learned that he was a Hungarian national and loaded. He was only thirty-two years old and had made a name for himself as a financer of several successful films and, as such, the top directors and actors in Hollywood had become chummy with him, hoping he would invest in one of their projects.

According to Wikipedia, Laverany wasn't exactly a self-made man. His grandfather was tied to the commies before, during, and after the failed '56 revolution and had made a small fortune confiscating the wealth of those who disagreed with party politics. Hollywood was the perfect place for someone like Laverany.

I looked down, and my beer was finished. I assumed that at least twenty minutes had passed. I went to pull out my cell phone to see where Natalie was, and it was then that I realized

I was having trouble moving my arms, which panicked me. I tried to stand, but my legs wouldn't respond. Molly passed my table with a tray of food, and I tried to call out to her, but found I couldn't speak. Although I was feeling very woozy, my mind was still coherent enough to realize I had been drugged.

"Well, well. I see the cat has got your tongue." I looked up, and saw that it was that creepy young PI, Evan Andrews. "You mind if I sit?" he said pointing to the empty seat. "I'll take that as a 'yes,'" he sneered when I couldn't reply.

"I imagine you saved this seat for Natalie. But here's a little secret, just between us guys," he said with a whisper, sitting down. "Natalie's not coming tonight. When we sent you the message that she was running late, we also sent her a message on your behalf, saying you had to cancel because something had come up."

I couldn't help but feel like a fool. If she was running late, why call the restaurant to tell me? Why not call me directly on my phone? I should have sensed the setup.

"I hope you're up for a short trip," said Andrews. "Because we're about to leave now."

The last words I remembered before it all went blank was Andrews saying, "I'm going to love what happens to you, especially after the way you and your partner treated me the other day. It cost me $2,500 and a day in a dentist's chair to save that tooth."

When I regained consciousness, I had a pounding headache and at first my eyes couldn't focus. But even in this rough state, I immediately recognized the unmistakable voice of Cy Green saying, "I believe our guest is about to join us in the land of the conscious." Each syllable he uttered felt like someone was playing very loud tom-toms in my skull.

It took me a few more minutes to shake out the cobwebs and figure out that I was in Cy Green's living room, and that my host was joined by Evan Andrews. I tried to move but couldn't. At first I thought that the drug I had been slipped was still in effect. After gaining a little more of my wits, I realized I was tied to a chair with my hands bound behind the back.

"How long have I been out?" I asked.

"Only a few hours," said Cy. Up close, even though it seemed impossible, Cy was even fatter than he appeared in pictures. He was wearing a ridiculous white suit with a red bow tie, and I wasn't sure if it was the chemicals still floating around in my brain, but he reminded me of a Macy's Thanksgiving parade-style balloon of a giant bowling pin.

"You, young man, have been very naughty. I believe you have something of mine, and I want it back." Cy leaned into within inches of my face to help make his point.

"Oh yeah, well, if I do have something of yours, I hope it's a new suit because what you're wearing looks preposterous."

Cy tilted his head back and gave a throaty laugh. "Mr. Trowbridge, you amuse me, but at the moment the only thing I care about is getting Mr. MacGuffin back. If you don't tell me where it is, I can assure you your future will be quite bleak."

"Last I knew MacGuffin was with a friend of mine, Bert Thompson. Only problem is that Bert is lying in the city morgue with a toe tag and at the moment is going by the name of John Doe. What I do know, however, is I suspect you knew my friend planned to steal MacGuffin, and you hired this clown PI," I said, nodding my head at Andrews, "to follow Bert around town and figure out what was going on. My guess is that he saw an opportunity, killed Bert while he was alone, and is going to fence MacGuffin to the highest bidder."

.".. Green was obese and obscenely so, with most of his weight hanging off his belly. He had a shock of gray hair, parted on the side, that was so vibrant it screamed white instead of gray, which was in contrast to his beady brown eyes."

"Hey," said Andrews indignantly. The PI came up to me and made a fist like he was going to sock me in the face as I sat bound to the chair. My legs were free, so before he could throw a punch, I kicked him hard in the shin. He yelped, and Cy Green let out another deep, guttural laugh.

"I thought of that possibility, Mr. Trowbridge," said Cy dismissively. "But frankly, Mr. Andrews isn't bright enough to pull something like that off. So, you're telling me Bert Thompson is dead and doesn't have what I want, and I'm telling you Mr. Andrews isn't smart enough to have it. By process of elimination that leaves only you." The smile was gone from his face, and he added sternly, "I want it back and I want it back now." His beady brown eyes bore in on me sharply.

"Why in the world do you even want the damn thing?" I asked.

Cy looked disappointed in me, and for a second I thought he was going to fly into a rage, but then he composed himself and looked serene. "For what it represents, of course. Valentino was the greatest star of his era, and he represented male sexuality at its rawest during a time when such things couldn't be discussed. And, after all, what is male sexuality, Mr. Trowbridge, but the ultimate fulfillment of greed, lust, and power?

"Imagine the history MacGuffin has been a part of. This Hollywood memento, the most unique collectible in the world I might add, was the talk of Hollywood parties during the golden age of film-making. If MacGuffin could talk, what stories he would tell!"

"You do know you're referring to a plaster of Paris penis?" I cut in sarcastically.

"No. It is more than that," rebuffed Green emphatically. "It disappeared in 1968 under the most unusual of circumstances, as I'm sure you are probably aware, which only adds to its value and mystique. After Pedro Noboa's murder, MacGuffin hadn't been seen for years, and people assumed it was lost forever. Some historians started to question whether it had ever existed at all. MacGuffin became my quest, my Holy Grail. I invested millions to track it down and followed every lead, no matter how ridiculous or improbable. I finally trailed MacGuffin down to an exotic trader in Cairo, Egypt of all places. When it came into my possession it was the happiest day of my life."

Cy Green turned away from me and held his hands behind his back as he added in that famous voice of his, "I want it back, Mr. Trowbridge, and 'no' isn't the appropriate answer."

"No," I said defiantly.

Turning around surprisingly briskly for such a heavy man, Cy looked at me thoughtfully. "You have twenty-four hours to return to me what is rightfully mine, no questions asked. If not, tomorrow will be the last sunrise you will ever see." He paused, and I thought he was done. "Oh, and one more thing, Mr. Trowbridge. If I ever see you within a mile of my daughter again, I'll personally rip your balls off."

Cy Green turned to Andrews, "Will you escort Mr. Trowbridge out of the building? I'm going to bed for the night."

"With pleasure," said the PI with a sneer. With that, Cy Green nodded politely at both of us and took his leave, waddling down the hallway.

When Cy was out of sight, and we'd heard the click of what I assumed was his bedroom door, Andrews turned to me and said, "Before I untie you, I owe you one thing—let's see how many teeth this loosens." With that he gave me his best right hook across my jaw, sending me and the chair I was tied to tumbling to the floor.

Chapter Nine

Shortly after sunrise I woke up in Natalie's bed. She lay naked on top of the covers and was in a deep sleep. I took a long look at that angelic face and heavenly body. If this was to be my last sunrise I might as well enjoy the view. Maybe Cy was right, and male sexuality was the ultimate fulfillment of greed, lust, and power, but there was something both masculine and quite right about feeling this way in the arms of a beautiful woman. This is the stuff that dreams are made of.

After getting tossed out of the high rise by Evan Andrews, I had checked my voice mail and saw that while I had been blacked out Natalie had left me a message. She was worried about the emergency that had caused me to cancel our date. I called her back and told her I was right outside her building. She promptly buzzed me in.

On the seventeenth floor she had coffee and a sympathetic ear waiting. I took a calculated risk, knowing I didn't have many cards to play, and told her the truth, the whole truth, and nothing but the truth. I started with my writing partnership with Bert Thompson ten years ago and ended with the threats from Cy minutes ago. I didn't apologize for my stupidity in getting involved in this mess, but I did say I wasn't proud of how I had been talked into it.

Pure Natalie, she was easy to talk to. When I was done she said, "If anyone is going to get their balls ripped off it will be

Cy, by me." Her blue eyes had become ice cold, and it looked like she meant every word of it.

She gave me a reassuring kiss on the cheek. "Look, about Cy," she said. "One thing I learned is not to worry about his threats. He's not going to kill you or anyone else. Cy Green! Big Hollywood director of horror flicks! Sometimes he acts like life is a plot in one of his movies, but when push comes to shove, he is mostly hot air."

"So, are we OK?" I asked.

"We are fine," Natalie replied and cuddled up next to me. "In fact, I'm glad that horrible thing is gone. It was a perverted phallic symbol that represented everything wrong with Hollywood. And to think my own father kept it in a place of honor in his home, not caring how it made women, or his own daughter for that matter, feel when visiting him. It makes me sick just thinking about it. Now I can only hope that whoever took it threw it into the harbor, so I never have to see the horrible thing again."

We talked some more before we trailed off to the bedroom. It was not exactly great foreplay, but Natalie added while unbuttoning her blouse, "With a dead body involved you'll need some help. I have a friend who is a crackerjack attorney. If you don't mind, I'll give her a call on your behalf in the morning."

I didn't mind. Nor did I mind how the rest of the night went.

But now I was awake and my cell phone was rattling, so I quickly grabbed it and left the bedroom so as not to wake Natalie. Dan was on the line.

"Where are you?" he asked.

"You don't want to know."

He really didn't, and he was smart enough not ask again. Instead he said, "I have some news, and most of it is not good."

"Go ahead," I replied, bracing myself for the worse.

"The police have figured out that the stiff is Bert Thompson. They also determined he was killed by a 9mm Ruger, the kind of gun first-time gun owners buy for protection. Because of that, they aren't treating Thompson's murder as a professional hit."

"Anything else?"

"They haven't tied Bert back to you yet, but you know as well as I do that it will only be a matter of time. If you have a plan, you better put it in motion now."

"I do," I replied, "but I'll need your help."

"I'm all ears."

My plan wasn't really a plan, more of a hope. That afternoon I left a message with Cy that I had important information on Mr. MacGuffin and I needed to see him, and that he should have Evan Andrews on hand as well.

*****

Cy opened the door himself when I arrived and greeted me with an impatient, "Well?"

"All in good time, big man," I said, pushing my way into the apartment.

Andrews was seated in the living room and looked me over nervously. His wild eyes were back. Nodding hello to him I said, "I owe you one from last night. And you can bet I always repay a debt."

The young PI looked scared, like he knew I meant it. I could see the wheels spinning in his head as he searched for a snappy comeback. Fortunately, Cy's phone rang, saving me from a continued back-and-forth with Andrews. As planned, Randy at the lobby's concierge desk was on the other line. Cy's voice was crisp and clear, but fueled with outrage as he blurted out, "What do you mean I have guests in the front lobby who say Mr. Trowbridge told them they could come up?" Cy looked at me sourly, but then he relented and said to the concierge, "Alright, fine. They are clear to come up."

Cy gave me the stink eye and said softly but firmly enough that it seemed more like a scream, "I made a promise to you, Mr. Trowbridge. If I don't have MacGuffin back by sunrise, you'll take a permanent swim in the harbor."

"Now, don't make any promises you can't keep," I chided. "I'm the only hope you have of finding your twisted collectible that means the world to you, and as long as that is the case you won't harm a hair on my head." Cy took this in and, I swear, he physically shrank as it sunk in that I was correct. Out of the corner of my eye, I could see that Andrews was about to protest that he, too, might be able to find MacGuffin. However, before he could speak, the doorbell rang, sparing us all his bullshit.

Dan walked in first. If the shit hit the fan, I wanted someone who I could count on backing me up. Next, Peter Laverany came in. "You!" bellowed Cy when he saw Laverany.

Laverany wore a tightly tailored mod suit that showed off his youthful, slim build and made him look like an extra on an *Austin Powers* movie set. He gently stroked the lapels of his jacket and looked around Cy's living room with a jaundiced eye before declaring with his one-of-a-kind accent, "I should have known someone like you would be living in a garish penthouse like this."

Cy lunged forward, but before the men could come to blows I separated them, saying, "I take it you both know each other." This was a safe assumption on my part. Hollywood was still, at the end of the day, a small, tight-knit community.

My plan was to get all the people who had a motive for killing Bert Thompson together in the same room, and get them talking to see what shook out. Cy took the bait immediately. "I approached our so-called guest once about investing in one of my movies. He turned me down. Too bad. If he had invested, his return would have been close to four hundred percent."

"I invest in art, not crap," said Laverany, who, standing next to Cy looked like Stan Laurel to Cy's Oliver Hardy.

"You know nothing about art or filmmaking," Cy countered. "You're just an insufferable little boy playing with daddy's money."

"Boys," I scolded. "We can have this battle of the wits later. I've gotten us all together to discuss something near and dear to your hearts: the whereabouts of Mr. MacGuffin and who he rightfully belongs to."

Turning to me, Laverany said, "Where is Mr. MacGuffin? The only reason I came today is because that man," he said, pointing at Dan, "told me you had him."

"In good time," I replied. "Can we all grab a seat? I have a few questions first, and we might as well be comfortable." Staring each other down, Cy Green and Laverany finally relented and slowly found seats, joining Evan Andrews. Dan and I remained standing.

Turning to Laverany I asked, "When did you first decide to steal MacGuffin?"

"'Steal' is such an ugly term, don't you think?" he asked. He looked around for a sympathetic face, and when he couldn't find one, he continued. "I'm a legitimate businessman. About seven years ago, Mr. Green was looking for financing for his last disgraceful slasher movie and invited me over to his Hollywood Hills house for the sales pitch. After hearing him tell me about it, I had absolutely no interest in the movie, and he served me the most god-awful petit fours in the process.

My night at Mr. Green's home wasn't a total loss, however; he took me on a private tour of his collectibles. When I saw Mr. MacGuffin, I knew I had to have him at all costs."

At this point Dan interrupted and asked, "Why?" This was out of character for Dan, who was usually the strong silent type. Everyone in the room somehow sensed that Dan chose his words sparingly, and a tension hung in the air until Laverany answered.

"My dear man," Laverany turned to Dan with pity, unable to fathom how sad it must be not to have the same egalitarian tastes as him. "Rudolph Valentino was the greatest male sex symbol Hollywood ever produced. He could seduce with his eyes at a glance. When the silent era ended and the actors could talk, sensuality lost something on screen that it could never get back. Did you know that when Valentino died 100,000 women rioted outside his funeral and several women committed suicide? Anything that powerful is something I want. No. Check that. Something I have to have."

Dan looked at Laverany like he was sorry he asked. To keep the ball rolling I asked, "And then what?"

"And then I made him an offer he couldn't refuse, but he did."

"And then he wouldn't take no for an answer," Cy interrupted. "For the next five years he hounded me with more offers and more money. I was sick of him. When I left Hollywood and didn't hear from him, I thought I was done with our little visitor for good."

"So…" I said, slowly putting two and two together, "when Cy refused to sell you MacGuffin and moved 3,000 miles away, you decide to steal it?"

Laverany nodded yes, totally unashamed by his admission.

"And how did Bert Thompson get mixed up in all this?" I asked.

"Because he was the right type of desperate," Laverany countered. "He was looking for funding for some ridiculous project of his. I wanted no part of it, but one could sense a pitiful desperation from Mr. Thompson. I could tell that he needed to do this project so bad he would do anything for it, and I mean anything.

"Let me explain something to you about Hollywood, Mr. Trowbridge. Desperation is its most abundant commodity. It is everywhere. People will do anything for the mere hope of success. Anything. When you have that power over someone—to make them lie, cheat, steal, murder, prostitute themselves, you name it—they will do it."

I had lived the life and knew what he was saying was true. What would I have given ten years ago just to have a buffoon like Cy Green meet with me to discuss a script I was working on?

"And how did you know someone was trying to steal MacGuffin from you?" I asked, turning to Cy Green.

"Because my disgusting little friend is right. Hollywood is a small, dirty place, where desperation is king and people would sell their first born for the hope of success. Not more than five minutes after he made a deal with you know who," barked Cy, pointing at Laverany. "Bert Thompson called me. He told me he wouldn't steal Mr. MacGuffin from me if I paid him. He said he needed money for a new project. It wasn't blackmail, he said, but an investment. As soon as his new project came to the big screen, I'd get all my money back and then some, and I wouldn't have to worry about him hiring someone to steal MacGuffin."

At this Peter Laverany let out a tsk-tsk sound, disappointed in my old friend, Bert, for not displaying honor among thieves.

"I, of course, turned him down," continued Cy.

"But now you were tipped off that a theft was possible," I said, speculating. "And you hired a PI firm to follow Bert Thompson and stop him."

"Had I insisted on a more senior member of the agency, we wouldn't be sitting here today," said Cy looking sharply at Evan Andrews.

"Hey!" said the PI in protest.

"Shut up!" countered Cy, causing Andrews to retreat like a kicked dog.

And just then it clicked. I knew who killed Bert Thompson and I knew what had happened to MacGuffin—at least I was pretty sure that I knew.

Chapter Ten

As I was going down on the elevator, I pictured Dan back in the penthouse apartment, doing his best to hold that mob at bay after I left abruptly, telling them I'd be right back.

Getting off on the seventeenth floor and taking a deep breath, I gave Natalie's door a hard knock. She answered, wearing black yoga pants and a tight red T-shirt; as usual, she looked fantastic. She didn't seem surprised to see me, but wore an expression like she had been expecting me and simply said, "Come on in."

We naturally gravitated to her breakfast nook and sat down on a pair of stools. From her nook was a floor to ceiling view of the harbor. In the distance, I could see a water taxi heading from one end to the other.

Reading my face, she asked, "Am I in trouble?"

"I think we both are," I replied, and she nodded solemnly, taking this in.

"How do you know Bert Thompson?" I asked.

"Thompson?" she shrugged. "I was hoping you would never ask."

She pouted and looked through me with those piercing blue eyes. But she went on calmly, "When Cy was in New York to receive yet another lifetime achievement award or whatever, he asked me to stop by his place once a day to make sure everything was in order. Lo and behold, the first day I checked in, I noticed broken glass on the floor and saw that god-awful penis had been taken. After inspecting the apartment, I couldn't find anything else that was missing. I was both relieved and thrilled someone had pinched MacGuffin.

"My celebration was short-lived when Cy's land line started to ring. Who has a land line anymore?" she asked incredulously. "Only old farts, like Cy," she answered herself.

"I picked up and answered, and it was your friend Bert on the line. Somehow, he had gotten Cy's home number. I told him Cy was out and wouldn't be back for several days and that I'm Cy's daughter. And you know what? Your friend was a pompous chauvinist," she added sharply.

I nodded, guessing that now wasn't the best time to go over Bert's pros and cons with her.

"You know what happened next?" she asked.

"Knowing Bert," I said, "he negotiated with you. He played both sides against the middle to see who would give him the best deal."

Natalie pointed at her nose to tell me I was right on target. "He thought that since I was a Green, I would want the damn thing back. At first, I was going to tell him to shove it. But then I calculated that if I turned him down, he would eventually get to Cy who would agree to buy it back, and that horrible dildo would be back on display. I was so close now to getting that awful object out of my life, I decided I was going to do what I could to make sure that didn't happen."

Natalie stood up now, and she must have been stressed because her English accent was thicker than normal. "I offered him a million and a quarter to buy it back. He gave me a time and place to meet for the transaction, stating that if I didn't have the money, he would pursue getting in touch with Cy. Of course, I don't have that type of money, but my plan was to talk to him and convince him to do the right thing and destroy MacGuffin, or at the very least take the original offer and be done with it."

"So why kill him?" I ask.

"How did you know?" she replied.

"The gun was a 9mm Ruger. A small gun," I added. "Just the type of weapon a woman would carry if she were heading to a shaky Baltimore neighborhood at night and was worried about her personal safety."

Natalie nodded that I was right, and her confession crushed me. Perhaps I should have figured out long ago that Natalie had done it, going all the way back to the second I felt Bert's body going cold in the alley. But until now I had held out hope that there was another explanation. And that is what love will do to you. Love will take logic and twist it like a pretzel even when the obvious truth is staring you in the face.

"As you can guess, our discussion in the alley didn't go well. I begged him to leave both me and Cy alone and do whatever he wanted with MacGuffin as long as Cy could never find it again. Bert was mad at me for wasting his time and yelled at me. I took it to a point, but when he called me 'girlie,' I guess I snapped. I pulled out the Ruger and demanded he hand the dildo over. I was going to take that preserved bit of Hollywood memorabilia and destroy it. He didn't take me seriously and laughed at me right before I pulled the trigger."

Natalie reflected on her mental image of the scene and added, "He should have taken me seriously."

"Is it safe to assume you then took Mr. MacGuffin and threw him in the harbor?"

"And how did you know that, too?" she asked again.

"Because last night you told me that you hoped whoever had it would throw it in there."

Natalie smiled warily, impressed with my detective skills. "So, what do we do now?" she asked. "You're not going to turn me in, are you?"

"We're talking about murder," I responded flatly. "Bert had his flaws, but he wasn't a monster. He was my former partner, and maybe we didn't have the type of success I had hoped for, but I owe someone who was a partner of mine a bit more than just walking away from his murder."

Silence hung in the air until Natalie filled the void. "Look. This is Baltimore, and they have more unsolved murders than police. If we hang tight, I bet they never solve this and eventually we'll be in the clear."

"Natalie," I interrupted.

Natalie snapped her finger and enthusiastically added, "I know! If the police ever ask, we can alibi each other and say we were together at the time of Bert's death. Or, I can say he tried to rape me in the alley, and it was self-defense."

"Natalie," I said more sternly.

Natalie's blue eyes were now rimmed with tears. "Trow," she said earnestly. "This is about more than just getting me off. I can't go through this again. I told you only a half of the truth about why I came down from New York to be with my father. The other part I didn't tell you was that a man I had loved for five years left me. It devastated me completely to love so deeply and then to lose it all. I thought I'd never get over it, until I met you. Please don't do this to me, to us. I know that we are just getting to know each other, but I think you feel it, too. We were made to be together. We aren't bad people, just flawed. Together—who knows—we just might be OK."

"I understand," I said, with a lump growing in my throat.

Natalie reached out and cradled my hands in hers, saying, "Please, Trow, tell me you won't turn me in."

Chapter Eleven

Dan and I were in a holding cell in central booking. A few hours before, we were outfitted with orange jumpsuits, and if we were lucky, we would get a preliminary hearing in the morning where bail would be set.

"Look at the bright side," said Dan. "They already dropped the theft charge, and if you cooperate, they'll also drop the aiding and abetting in a homicide. What does that leave them? A lousy breaking and entering rap for busting into Cy Green's place. A B&E charge in Baltimore is nothing. We'll be out before the Orioles' opening day."

Dan chowed down a baloney sandwich. We had been incarcerated for two meals so far, and we had gotten the same horrible white bread and baloney sandwiches each time. I refused to eat, so Dan took my sandwich, and also the one of a strung-out junkie we shared the cell with. So far Dan was six sandwiches in and seemed quite content.

"Even if I get a slap on the wrist," I said, "they'll take my PI's license away from me. What am I going to do when I get out?"

Dan shrugged and added optimistically, "Baltimore is for the taking. A couple of sharp guys like us? There are a million angles we can play. Something tells me we are going to be more than fine."

"Next you'll be telling me this is the beginning of a beautiful friendship."

"Nope," said Dan, who finished up the sandwich with one last big bite, "I'm telling you it's been a beautiful friendship since the first grade, and now we are just starting a new chapter."

I had to admit that there was something very Zen about Dan; nothing ever seemed to faze him. The lawyer who Natalie had called for me just yesterday was obviously out of the question now, but Dan swore he knew a friend of a friend whose brother was a lawyer and he would help us out. Best of all, this lawyer was tight with a lot of the judges in town, and his clients usually got an easier ride in court.

"Trowbridge!" a young hefty female African American prison guard yelled as she approached. "The detective wants to talk to you."

I stood up as she fished for her keys to let me out. Dan winked at her and said, "Someone is looking good today." She smiled back and my gut told me that Dan had just earned some extra baloney sandwiches the next time the meal cart wheeled around.

I was marched down a long corridor that led to one of the interrogation rooms where I was locked in and told to wait. When the guard took off the handcuffs, she asked, "Your friend, does he have a girl?"

"Not sure," I answered honestly, "but I may be available, as I'm pretty sure my girlfriend is furious with me for ratting her out." The guard laughed at that and then said something to the effect that there could be no future between us, as bringing home a white boy would be the death of her mother. The guard laughed at that as well. I was glad my trials and tribulations were bringing joy to someone.

I stewed alone in the interrogation room for a long while. It's an old police tactic. Eventually Detective Jones came into the room, throwing open the door with a loud bang. Jones was about my age, black, with a clean-shaven head. He was one of those homicide detectives who thought being a snappy dresser made him look smarter. Unfortunately for Jones, his sartorial sense was a little off and his tie clashed badly with his suit jacket, loud enough to give me a headache.

Jones was carrying a manila envelope. In it was a thirty-page handwritten document authored by me. This was the confession that I had written shortly after telling the Baltimore PD about Natalie Green, Bert Thompson, and Mr. MacGuffin.

Jones flopped the confession down in front of me and asked, "You ready to sign it?"

I nodded and replied, "Just let me read it over one last time, and add a little more about what's happened since we last spoke."

"You know it doesn't have to be a novel," he said sternly.

"I just want to be accurate. I owe that to posterity."

"Posterity?" laughed Jones as if the word on its own was one of the great punch lines ever. But I meant what I had said, and as a former writer I thought a clear paper trail penned by my own hand would best describe what I did and why. If you are reading this, then my instincts have been justified. What you are reading is my final confession.

"You know," Jones said seriously after his laughter trailed off. "Between you and me, thank you. The DA will never tell you this, but we didn't have much on the Bert Thompson murder. You may have saved me months of legwork, and even at that I'm not sure what I could have dug up would have led me to Natalie Green. The DA owes you one. When this all shakes out, I wouldn't be surprised if you and your friend got nothing more than time served."

The mere mention of Natalie's name made my heart skip. "And how is Natalie?"

"Refusing to talk without a lawyer. Hers is due to arrive any moment, and then I'll take a crack at her. But she is pretty much cooked. Between your confession and the fact that we located the Ruger with her prints on it, she is toast, lawyer or no lawyer."

I nodded and asked, "How much time do you think she'll get?"

Jones looked thoughtfully and said, "In the good old days, she would have gotten the chair. But these days, and with deep pockets and high-priced lawyers and no priors, she'll probably get twenty years. With good behavior, she could be out in ten."

I processed this and did the math, calculating how old both of us will be in ten years. "Can you do me a favor?"

"What's that?" asked Jones tentatively.

"When you see Natalie, tell her no matter what, I still love her and hope she forgives me for turning her in. And no matter how long the sentence, when her time is up, I'll be waiting for her."

Jones nodded solemnly, not sure what to make of that. He left shortly afterwards, probably to meet with Natalie and her lawyer. After he had gone, I read through my confession one last time. For the record, let me state clearly that this confession is of my own free will.

About the Author

Matthew Kastel lives in an undisclosed location in suburban Maryland with his beloved black lab, Hershey…and the rest of his family.

Enjoyed this story? Read more from Frayed Edge Press...

Literature

Ambushing the Void short stories by James McAdams
*¿Cómo Hacer Preguntas? or How To Make Questions: 69 Instructional
   Poems (in English)* by Daniel Hales
Bellapalma by Jens Bjørneboe; translated by Esther Greenleaf Mürer
Ere the Cock Crows by Jens Bjørneboe; translated and with a
   reconstruction of the play by Esther Greenleaf Mürer
Rape Jokes by Louise MacGregor
Stealing: A Novel in Dreams by Shelly Brivic
The Splooge Factory poety by Christina Springer

History and Politics

*"Do Not Misunderstand Me": The Collected Radical Addresses to the
   Unity Congregation (1888-1891)* by Hugh Owen Pentecost
Jeremiah Hacker: Journalist, Anarchist, Abolitionist by Rebecca
   Pritchard
A Nurse's Story: Medical Missionary in Korea and Siberia, 1915-1920 by
   Delia Battles Lewis

Street Smart Series -- Short Fiction for People on the Go

Full Fare by Jean-Bernard Pouy
Down and Out in Paris, with Cat by R.A. Bolo
The Accidental Anarchist by A.R. Melnik
Stealing MacGuffin by Matthew Kastel
Pele's Domain by Albert Tucher

Visit us at: https://www.frayededgepress.com/

www.ingramcontent.com/pod-product-compliance
Lightning Source LLC
Chambersburg PA
CBHW070914100726
47907CB00008B/2316